I0551514

CINDY LEFEVRE

Solara of Sardon
Born of War. Bound by Light.

Copyright © 2025 by Cindy LeFevre

All rights reserved. No part of this publication may be reproduced, stored or transmitted in any form or by any means, electronic, mechanical, photocopying, recording, scanning, or otherwise without written permission from the publisher. It is illegal to copy this book, post it to a website, or distribute it by any other means without permission.

This novel is entirely a work of fiction. The names, characters and incidents portrayed in it are the work of the author's imagination. Any resemblance to actual persons, living or dead, events or localities is entirely coincidental.

First edition

ISBN. 979 8-9996036-0-9

This book was professionally typeset on Reedsy.
Find out more at reedsy.com

For all children who see light in the darkest forests, and for those who guide them home.

Foreword

The Waiting Star

There are places beyond stars.
Worlds the maps have forgotten.
In one of them, the last warrior of a dying world waits.
She listens not for war, but for a whisper.
Because sometimes, destiny arrives not as a roar,
but as a child's cry in the dark.
And when that call comes…
She rides.

Preface

The Stars Remember...

Long before Solara was born, before the fall of Sardon's great cities, a council of warrior-seers stood beneath a dying moon and saw a vision.

A child — small, alone, cloaked in winter sorrow — called out through time.

A stallion of starlight thundered across galaxies.

And a blade of memory, buried far from home, would rise again.

Knowing they could not stop what was to come, the women of Solara's bloodline forged a living sword born of pure magic.

They named it Starcleave — but it began not as steel, but as a seed.

Infused with their voices, their pain, and their strength, they sent it through a rift — across stars, through dimensions — to Earth.

It fell into a forest, where the trees were old and magic still lingered in the soil; it slept.

By Cindy LeFevre

PART 1: THE BEGINNING

Chapter 1 - Solara's Arrival

Solara of Sardon is not just a warrior — she is the last flame of her line. A rider of cosmic winds, bearer of deep scars, and guardian of forgotten children. Her white stallion, Uno, is no ordinary beast. He is born of Sardon's celestial herds — intelligent, proud, and woven with ancient light.

When Solara sees the vision of Earth's children, it is the pain of one small girl that pierces her: Lena.

Snow. Silence. The hollow ache of being unseen.

The girl's pain becomes a beacon.

Solara steps into the portal — a radiant stone carved with ancient glyphs — and reaches for Uno.

She has only a heartbeat. They vanish together.

The Colorado mountains, cloaked in winter. Icy wind howled. Trees swayed. Solara landed hard in the snow.

The air was heavy with silence, but it was not empty. The

wind carried scents Solara had never known—pine, frost, and something deeply alive. She looked around in wonder. This world pulsed with slow, rooted strength. The stars above were familiar, yet the ground beneath her feet hummed with something new. She reached out and touched a branch, feeling the quiet wisdom in its bark. Earth was different from Sardon— less radiant, more grounded—but it listened. And it was listening now.

* * *

Chapter 2 - Lena: The Hidden Ember

Eight-year-old Lena is small, quiet, and far older than she should be. She comes from the Veilblood, a lineage of women who can walk between light and shadow, call to animals, and feel the earth in their bones.

Her mother, Alenya, was the last true Veilwalker — a healer who lived hidden in a quiet town. Her father was once a guardian too… until he turned to darkness. He betrayed Alenya, demanding Lena's growing power.

Alenya gave her life to protect Lena. With her final breath, she sealed the child's magic and sent her away — through a portal of frost and breath — to a cabin deep in the Colorado woods, to live with a woman named Marrow.

Marrow is cold, silent, cruel in her stillness. She says little, but her magic fills the cabin like smoke. The air is thick with binding spells and dead charms.

But the forest remembers Lena's blood.

And the animals come.

A red fox with a torn ear. A silent raven. And a hare named

Bran, who speaks without speaking — in riddles and rhythms.

"You are the last ember," Bran once told her. "And embers grow teeth when the wind is right."

Around her neck hangs a pendant, strung on a thin leather cord — green stone, worn smooth with age, etched faintly with the image of a warrior on horseback beneath a full moon. It once belonged to her mother, and though Marrow has tried to take it, Lena never lets it leave her skin.

She doesn't know what it does.

Only that it hums quietly when the wind moves through the trees.Lena walks the forest edge every day. Never too far.

But far enough to listen.

One night, she places her hand on a stone under the hearth — one that pulses softly with warmth. She doesn't speak.

She feels. And somewhere beyond the stars… Solara hears.

* * *

Chapter 3 – Lucy: The Guardian at the Edge of the Wild

* * *

The forest was too quiet.

Lena had wandered farther than ever before — not by choice, but because Marrow's anger had filled the cabin like smoke. She'd run. Tears froze on her cheeks. Her boots slipped on the snow-covered stones.

Then she heard it.

A sharp bark. Quick and sure.

She turned, and out of the trees came a small white dog, coat bristling, eyes bright with purpose. She moved like a flash of lightning — low to the ground, nose twitching, alert. A Jack Russell, though Lena didn't know the name. Just the feeling:

Safe. Brave. Here.

The dog barked once, sharply. Then turned and looked back, tail high.

Lena hesitated.

Bran had told her, "When your courage fades, follow the one who walks without fear."

So she did.

The dog's name, she would learn later, was Lucy — a guardian sent by fate or forest, it didn't matter. From that moment, Lucy never left her side.

She chased off dark shapes. Found hidden paths. And when Lena feared she'd be lost forever, it was Lucy who led her toward starlight — and toward Solara.

* * *

Chapter 4 – Uno and the Council of the Wild

* * *

Uno senses her before Solara does — the girl's light. Her sadness. Her pull.

As he steps deeper into the forest, the animals come.

A raven lands above.

"Stranger of the sky," it cries. "Beast not born of this soil!"

A black fox paces the ridge, tail flicking in distrust.

Uno bows his head and exhales. From his breath, starlight spirals. Snow swirls. Time bends.

He shows them her:

Lena's light, the echo she left in him when she called.

Bran appears. "He carries her," the hare says. "She touched his heart before the veil broke."

"He smells like stars," the fox mutters. "But stars burn forests."

"And yet," Bran replies, "some stars warm the roots."

The animals watch. Wait. Then step aside. And they speak of a grove — one that holds something Solara will need.

* * *

Chapter 5 – The Grove of Breath and Bone

❧

Bran leads Uno and Solara to the edge of an ancient grove — silent, mist-shrouded, older than language. Snow does not fall here. The trees bend inward like guardians.

At its heart: a ring of roots. Coiled. Alive.

"The sword is here," Bran says. "But it sleeps. And it remembers."

Solara steps into the grove alone.

The moment her foot touches the soil, she vanishes from Earth.

* * *

She stands on a battlefield.

Sardon. Years ago.

Her sister Vessa is screaming. Fire falls from the sky. Solara is twelve again.

And she runs.

"You left her," the sword says. "You ran. This blade does not serve the guilty."

Solara falls to her knees. "I did. I was afraid."

Silence.

"I never stopped fighting. Not once. For every life I could reach. And I will not fail this child."

The field burns around her.

And then it is gone.

* * *

The grove returns.

The roots part.

The sword stirs — not fully formed, vines spiraling, its hilt more alive than forged. It glows faintly, pulsing with the earth's rhythm.

"You are worthy not because you are unbroken.

You are worthy because you chose to rise."

Only when the sword gently lifts toward her does she touch it—knowing it will not be whole until Lena completes it. The blade was seeded with the power of Sardon, but it needs the pulse of Earth to awaken fully. Lena, born of Veilblood and rooted in Earth's living rhythm, is that bridge. Her lineage carries the purity and balance of ancient Earth magic, and her soul remains untouched by the corruption that spreads through the world. Starcleave, though powerful, is incomplete without the grounding force of Earth—without Lena's calm to temper Solara's fire. Only through their union—star and soil, fire and breath—can the sword reach its true potential and fulfill the legacy it was born to carry.

Chapter 5 – The Grove of Breath and Bone

* * *

Chapter 6 – Lena: Trusting the Wild

Lena wakes to silence. Not fear — something else. Something shifting.

She and Lucy step outside.

The snow is soft. The trees hum.

The animals are waiting.

Bran speaks first. "The sword is awake."

Lena clutches her stone. "Who is she?"

"The one the stars remembered."

Lena doesn't understand. But she nods.

The fox steps forward and brushes her boot. The raven circles.

Inside, Marrow stirs. The fire flares green.

"Come with us," Bran says. "You are not forgotten."

And Lena — scared, shaking, but burning with quiet light — steps into the forest, Lucy by her side.

Toward her future.

Toward Solara. And the storm that is coming.

Chapter 6 – Lena: Trusting the Wild

* * *

PART 2: THE WHISPER BEYOND THE VEIL

Chapter 1 — The Wizard Who Waits

He felt the shift the moment it happened.

Far to the north, beyond all maps and memory, the sky rippled with something more ancient than wind. In a place where time hung still and color had long since faded, a figure stood atop the broken tower of Varkul — a monolith of obsidian that pierced the clouds like a blade.

He wore black robes that dragged like shadow behind him, woven with runes that pulsed faintly as though alive. The cold bent to him. The wind avoided him. Light dared not linger too long on his skin.

His name was Malrik.

Taker of souls.

Breaker of bonds.

The one who drinks from memory.

No kingdom claimed him, and none dared try. Cities that once resisted no longer breathed. The roots of the world twisted in his presence, and the air cracked with quiet despair wherever he passed.

And yet, tonight, something pressed back.

He had been crafting a soul trap—an arcane sphere of binding sorrow—when the tremor came. Not from the ground. Not from the wind.
From the fabric of the veil itself.

He turned sharply, his eyes like burned glass, and looked to the sky. Somewhere distant… something had crossed through. Something powerful. Something old.

A presence he had not tasted in centuries.

A warrior. A stallion. A seed awakened.

Malrik whispered to the void. It whispered back in a language only he remembered.

"A child of Sardon has come."

* * *

His lip curled.

He had long hunted the lost lines of Veilblood. Whispers, traces, half-forgotten names. He thought the last of them dead or powerless.

But now... something had bloomed.

He didn't know where the girl was—not yet—but she flickered now in his vision like a distant star. And beside her burned a light that made even his magic hesitate.

Uno. The White Flame.

And the rider of that light...

Solara.

He had heard that name once, drawn from the dying breath of a dreamwalker he consumed.

And now she was here. Not hidden.

Not quiet. Awake.

The hunter had crossed through. And the prey had not yet learned it was being hunted.

Malrik turned back to his chamber, where an ancient black map pulsed with veins of starlight and bone. His long fingers traced the shifting ley lines, watching the tears in the veil widen.

He would find her. He would tear her light from the earth. And he would unmake the sword before it ever bloomed.

* * *

Chapter 2 – The Outlier

Erik Halden sat alone in his high-tech cabin deep in the San Juan Mountains, the low hum of servers and the glow of monitors his constant companions. By trade, he was once a NOAA scientist-sharp-eyed, meticulous, and too curious for the comfort of his superiors. He'd asked questions that didn't fit the script, spotted anomalies others dismissed, and eventually, they let him go with a quiet handshake. It hadn't broken him. Instead, it had freed him. Now he ran his own models, monitored his own satellites, and answered to no one. but himself.

Home was more than the cabin. Just down the slope sat the farmhouse where his wife, Marian, tended their hives and gardens. Together they worked the land-raising bees, growing vegetables, coaxing life from the stubborn Southern Colorado soil. They were rooted and steady, the kind of people who could thrive through lean years and long winters. But there was an ache, unspoken yet always present-the child they had not been able to have. Marian rarely spoke of it, pouring her care instead into the bees, the earth, and the quiet rhythm of the farm. Erik felt it too, but he carried it differently, keeping his hands busy and his mind sharp.

That grounded life made what he saw on his screens that night all the more jarring. The spike appeared without warning. Not a storm. Not natural. Something else-something alive. His fingers flew across the keyboard, pulling heat maps, energy curves, electromagnetic pulses. The location made no sense: no structures, no installations. Just forest. And then, almost hidden in the noise, a second blip. He rewound the feed. Enhanced the image. Two spikes. One pure. One... corrupted. Erik reached for his encrypted comms, his voice low and certain. "Friends, we've got something."

Within minutes, a thread lit up. A physicist in New Mexico. A hacker in Canada. A botanist with an occultist streak in Portland. They weren't an official group. Just minds who never fit anywhere else. They called themselves The Outliers.

But Erik trusted two more than the rest: Tess, a climate scientist who had walked away from academia to build a lab in the desert, and Jonas, an engineer-turned-forager who knew how to disappear—and how to see what others missed.

Tess was already online. "That pulse wasn't solar," she said. "It's not matching any coronal event. But it's... rhythmic. Almost biological."

Jonas joined moments later, calm as always. "I've seen tree rings do this—when something happens to the planet. This is big, Erik."

Erik showed them the pulse, the trajectory. The anomaly.

One of the others—Ronan—tilted his head. "That's not just energy. That's intent."

The conversation turned. The occultist whispered of ancient convergence points, nodes of elemental power. The physicist asked about satellite tracking. Erik listened, compiled, calculated.

And then his wife walked in, barefoot and silent.

"You saw it, didn't you?" she said softly.

He nodded.

"Whatever it is," she said, "it's not coming. It's already here."

* * *

Chapter 3 – The Shadow Network

In the corners of the world untouched by sunlight, Malrik's reach was felt not through brute force—but through influence, corruption, and the slow erosion of truth.

Governments called it chaos. Economists labeled it instability. Scientists blamed random anomalies. But beneath the surface of modern systems pulsed the tendrils of something far older than logic.

Malrik.

He had no official name in modern society. But his agents—willing or unknowingly swayed—walked the halls of power. They pulled invisible strings from behind polished desks and sealed boardrooms.

There were senators who passed bills they didn't understand. Journalists who killed stories just before they broke. Military advisors who steered satellites away from certain coordinates with no explanation. And CEOs who funneled billions into defense technologies whose true designs were never revealed.

Each had felt a whisper—dark, persuasive, subtle.

"Do this, and you'll gain more than you lose."

A man named Clayburn at a northern intelligence station dismissed the faint blip picked up the same night as Erik Halden's discovery. He flagged it as solar interference and rerouted the signal path.

In London, a woman named Dr. Veldt ran an algorithm to purge an entire week's worth of cosmic monitoring data—data that had caught the exact moment Solara crossed over.

They were not possessed. They were influenced.

And influence was all Malrik required.

Back in Varkul, Malrik hovered over his obsidian map. Runes pulsed in sharp rhythm as connections activated across continents. A slow grin split his face.

"They do not know what they serve," he whispered.

But they would soon deliver what he needed.

The light had come. And the world, as it was, would begin to fracture from within.

* * *

PART 3: THE JOURNEY BEGINS

Chapter 1 – First Steps

* * *

Eight-year-old Lena sat on the edge of the hearthstone, her fingers curled around a smooth, pulsing rock buried just beneath the ash. The stone was warm. Alive. And though she didn't fully understand it, she could feel it listening.

Marrow was asleep in the back room, the door closed tight, the air thick with spells Lena had learned not to question. But tonight, the forest called more loudly than ever.

Lucy—a wiry little Jack Russell with the heart of a lion—was already waiting by the door, tail flicking, ears sharp. And eyes that said, Follow me.

Lena had never looked back.

Her mother was gone. Her father... a name never spoken. A shadow, not a memory.

But the forest remembered.

Bran, the hare with moonlit eyes, had whispered just last night: "The sword has woken. Time bends."

So Lena moved. Out the door. Through the snow. Lucy right behind.

The wild was waiting.

Far beyond, in a grove where no snow dared fall, Solara knelt before a ring of roots. Uno stood behind her, calm as the stars that once guided them. She reached not for the sword, but to connect to the hum beneath the ground.

Starcleave—the blade born of magic, not metal—slept still. Its vines twitched faintly, its hilt grown of living memory. The council of Sardon had sent it through as a seed, long before Solara's birth, knowing the world would one day need a light it could not forge.

And now, the grove stirred.

"You want to fight," Uno's gaze said, silent but sure.

Solara clenched her fists. "I must fight. Something dark is near."

"And yet," Uno seemed to reply, "you must also listen."

The sword responded to her presence—but not fully. Not yet. It waited for another.

The girl.

Lena.

They were linked. Earth to star. Flame to ember.

Solara rose, the earth's pulse steady beneath her feet. She would not draw the sword until it was whole. And it would only be whole when Lena touched it too.

Together, they would face the darkness.

Together, they would awaken the full power of Starcleave.

And together, they would remind the world what light truly was.

* * *

Solara of Sardon

Chapter 2 – Toward the Heartbeat

Solara moved like dusk in motion—steady, measured, deliberate. Uno guided her not with reins but with presence. He knew the path before her heart did. His patience was not passive; it was fierce and focused, a discipline drawn from ages of quiet watching. He taught Solara to slow her breath, to listen to the soil, to let the wind shape her direction rather than fight it. Where Solara burned with purpose, Uno cooled her edges. Where she longed to rush, he taught her the rhythm of the land.

Every step was a question. Every pause, an answer. Together, they moved closer—not just to Lena, but to the heartbeat of the Earth itself.

Far across the vast weave of forest and snow, Lena ran with Lucy at her heels. Or perhaps Lucy led. The little dog, small in size but great in spirit, carried the courage Lena didn't yet know she had. She barked when Lena hesitated. She waited when Lena faltered. And in her eyes burned a steady flame: We can do this.

Where Lena's legs trembled, Lucy's paws were sure. Where Lena feared what lay ahead, Lucy looked forward. Theirs was not a journey of strength alone, but of remembering—who they were, where they came from, and what was calling them forward.

As the Earth watched and the stars whispered, the two journeys pressed onward—unfolding, converging.

And the sword, Starcleave, stirred in its roots.

* * *

45

Chapter 3 – Mother Earth

Before time had names and seasons had cycles, she stirred.

Beneath roots and rivers, deeper than stone and storm, she hummed with ancient breath. Mother Earth was no figure of myth—she was the first memory, the keeper of balance, the breath between what was and what might be.

She did not speak in words, but in weather. She sighed in hurricanes, wept in floods, and cleansed in fire. She stitched the continents together with threads of energy, flowing unseen like rivers below rivers—channels of life, change, and restoration.

When the weight of greed pressed too deeply into her skin, she adjusted. When the breath of her forests grew thin with smoke, she opened chasms and summoned winds. Viruses, tremors, storms—none were vengeance. They were recalibrations.

Her aim was not wrath. It was balance.

Lena, even in her youth, felt it. Not in her ears, but in her bones. A rhythm pulsing beneath every footfall, every heartbeat. She didn't know the word for it, but she knew its truth.

And Solara—new to Earth, yet bound by its call—felt it too. Sardon's magic had been woven with starlight, fierce and radiant, but Earth's was deeper—rooted, humming with breath and cycles. Sardon had forged warriors; Earth nurtured guardians. In the silence between Uno's steps and the tremble of leaves before rain, Solara felt the difference. Earth didn't command. It listened. In the stillness before the wind turned.

Mother Earth moved not with haste, but with wisdom beyond centuries. She felt Lena's courage rise, Solara's fire steady, and the darkness gathering like a bruise.

She did not fear.

She watched. She remembered.

And as the two daughters of light took their first steps toward each other, Mother Earth stirred.

The rivers beneath rivers surged.

The balance had begun to shift to hope.

* * *

Chapter 4 – The Convoy

Far from forests and snow, in the pulsing heat of an abandoned airfield, the engines roared to life—low, guttural growls wrapped in matte-black steel. The convoy was moving. Not an army, but a storm. Dozens of vehicles—custom-built Nightfangs, rare armored SUVs with reinforced bodies and cloaked sensor arrays—lined up like silent predators. Sleek. Terrifying. Intimidatingly rare.

At their head, in a vehicle that looked less driven and more summoned, sat Malrik.

He didn't speak. He didn't need to. The men around him—hulking, red-eyed brutes in thick body armor and tactical gear—were not paid to think. They were trained to follow, to crush, to consume. He called them The Huskborn, empty of thought, full of violence. They were not born that way. They had once been men—soldiers, mercenaries, exiles. Malrik found them in moments of despair or rage, when their light had flickered low.

Through rituals older than language, he hollowed them out—stripping fear, memory, and mercy—leaving only obedience and wrath. Each one was enhanced with arcane sigils burned into their flesh and injected with a dark serum that dulled pain and amplified aggression. They did not speak unless commanded. They did not question. They did not stop. To the outside world, they looked like elite operatives. But they were no longer truly alive. They were vessels—malice in motion.

They were not magic. But Malrik's influence coiled in their veins, just beneath the skin.

And then there was Cassian Dregs, the mouth of the flame.

Cassian was everything the Huskborn were not—eloquent, poised, dangerous in ways no muscle ever was. His voice could ignite a riot or soothe a crowd. And he lived to serve Malrik's rise.

He stood atop the lead vehicle now, arms wide as the convoy rolled out.

Somewhere far ahead, in forests older than fire, Solara and Lena began to move toward each other. But darkness was not idle. Malrik was coming.

* * *

Chapter 5 – The Launch

The signal still echoed faintly across Erik's network as dawn crept down the mountain.

Erik stood outside his cabin with a thick field map in hand, boots crunching across frost-laced gravel. The coordinates weren't exact, but they narrowed the event down to a region—Southern Colorado, not far from the San Luis Valley.

"I'm going closer," Erik said over the open channel.

Tess's voice filtered through. "You're going to hike into a potential cosmic rift with a drone and a coffee thermos?"

"I've done dumber things with less gear," Erik replied.

Jonas joined the call, his voice unusually sharp. "Be cautious. That place is old. The veil is thinner there. If something entered, the residue could affect your perception."

"I'm not going in blind," Erik assured. "Just close enough to launch. I've got a terrain drone with a thermal sweep, quantum lensing, and EM echo capture. Should tell us what kind of disturbance we're dealing with."

He paused, then added, "I also rigged it to map ley flow—just in case you're right, Jonas."

Jonas was silent a moment, then: "Good."

Tess was already typing. "I'll monitor uplink from here. Keep your feed clean and encrypted. And Erik… be careful. We still don't know what that second signal really means."

Erik nodded to no one. "If it's Malrik, I want to know sooner rather than later."

He loaded the drone case into the back of his 4x4 and locked the equipment vault.

Above him, the wind stirred strangely.

He turned once, scanning the trees at the edge of his property. They were still. But something in the air felt… aware.

Erik climbed into the truck and started the engine.

The hunt was on.

* * *

PART 4: THE CONVERGENCE OF LIGHT

Chapter 1 – Meadow of First Light

The sun had just begun to crest the ridgeline, spilling golden ribbons across the high valley. Here, winter's final breath had yielded to the first warmth of spring. Snowmelt whispered beneath the soft moss, and a shallow pond mirrored the sky with glass-like stillness. Wildflowers stirred awake—spring buttercup bright as captured sunlight, alpine forget-me-not holding the hue of far-off skies, and early crimson paintbrush tipped as though the dawn itself had brushed past them. The breeze carried their scent like a quiet promise, weaving it into the heartbeat of the land.

It was a place untouched. Protected. Waiting.

Lena arrived first.

She stepped cautiously from the trees, her boots soaked from the stream bed below, her breath catching as she took in the sight. This meadow... it felt like a memory she never had, but somehow knew. Lucy trotted beside her, alert but calm, nose twitching at the sweet air.

Lena's heart pounded—not from fear, but from knowing something—*someone*—was coming.

Lena was a true empath. She felt the emotions of others as clearly as her own. The grief of a fallen tree, the joy of a singing bird, the tension hidden in a stranger's smile—all of it passed through her like music in the wind. And now, standing in this meadow, she felt the presence of someone powerful... and familiar.

Solara emerged across the field like a shadow turned light. She moved with the grace of someone born from stars, her cloak flowing behind her, her eyes wary but resolute. Uno followed, his hooves silent on the earth, every muscle tuned to the tension in the air. Solara carried Starcleave at her side—the sword alive with quiet power, its vines pulsing faintly with light.

They stopped at opposite edges of the meadow. Neither spoke.

They didn't need to.

Lucy and Uno moved first—without hesitation. The little terrier approached the great stallion with tail lifted high, and Uno bent his head gently, touching her nose with his. It was the kind of greeting beyond language. Recognition. Trust.

That moment shattered the stillness.

Solara took a step forward. So did Lena.

Solara's grip on the sword hilt loosened as she studied the small girl—mud on her coat, fire in her eyes. Lena stared up, not with awe, but with a quiet curiosity. She felt Solara. As if her bones knew her already.

"You're the one," Lena said softly.

Solara nodded. "And so are you."

Above them, the clouds parted to let more light through, and for a moment, the breeze circled around them in a spiral—petals lifting, grasses bending. The earth knew. The earth welcomed them.

Two hearts. Two paths.

One convergence.

And just beneath the ground, hidden in roots and magic, Starcleave began to hum again.

* * *

PART 5: THE RECKONING OF SHADOWS

Chapter 1 – The Edge of Light

* * *

The meadow was still alive with the echoes of unity—Starcleave glowing faintly in the hands of Solara and Lena. Birds chirped, petals danced, and for a heartbeat, everything held the silence of a promise fulfilled.

But there was no time for celebration.

A low rumble, not of thunder but of engines, approached from the south. The ground trembled beneath heavy wheels, and from the tree line emerged a convoy of hulking, black vehicles—Yukons, Marauders, and other unmarked monsters of metal and menace. They stopped in a clean, ominous line, their dark shells gleaming dully beneath the spring sun.

The driver's door of the lead vehicle opened.

Cassian Dregs stepped out.

He was tall, composed, and unnervingly confident—a man whose voice could stir crowds and whose eyes never blinked when lying. He wore a suit too perfect for the forest and carried the smile of someone who believed they were already winning.

He approached slowly, arms outstretched.

"We don't want conflict," he said. "Only a conversation."

Solara stepped forward, Starcleave humming in her hand. Its vines pulsed with silver light, wrapping gently up her arm.

"Then speak," she said.

Cassian tilted his head. "The sword is powerful. But power must be managed, directed, kept safe."

Solara said nothing.

"Give it to us," Cassian continued. "And no harm will come to the girl."

Lucy growled. Lena's hand clenched around her pendant. Uno took a single step forward, hooves pressing into the moss with deliberate weight.

Then Starcleave ignited.

Not with flame—but with radiant light. The vines curled upward, spiraling into the air, and the blade shimmered like dawn rising through fog.

Solara raised it and stepped forward.

The light touched Cassian's chest.

He froze.

And then, before their eyes, he changed. The sneer fell from his lips. His shoulders dropped. His gaze wavered.

Cassian Dregs began to cry.

Memories flooded him—things long buried, pieces of humanity twisted by ambition. He dropped to his knees, whispering

61

apologies, his voice raw with something he had forgotten: remorse.

From deep in the woods, Malrik felt it.

His scream cut across the land like a blade of ice.

* * *

Chapter 2 – Beneath and Above

Erik stood on a rocky overlook, breath caught in his chest as he watched through the drone feed. The sword, the man's transformation—every pixel recorded. He widened the satellite parameters, running heat and energy signatures, but the data didn't make sense. Spikes in the earth. Bursts of electromagnetic vibration. Something big was coming.

"I've never seen readings like this," he murmured into his headset.

Back at his off-grid cabin, through the network, his friends watched the feed in silence. The screen flickered.

"It's not just Earth," one of them said, the one with arcane tattoos traced into his arms. "It's consciousness. It's change."

Erik nodded. "And we're going to show the world."

In the meadow, Malrik appeared.

He stepped from shadow as if it bent for him, cloaked in robes that shifted like oil on water. His eyes found Lena immediately.

But Lena was no longer there.

She had vanished.

Only Lucy stood where the girl had been, teeth bared, body low.

Solara turned, ready to strike, but something stopped her.

A hum in the earth. A wind through the grass. The trees trembled.

And from the soil itself, Lena rose.

Her eyes were lit with green fire, and vines coiled gently around her arms.

She had become one with the forest.

"No," Malrik whispered. "This is not your world."

Lena didn't speak. She simply lifted her hand.

And the storm came.

Lightning cracked the sky. Rain poured in sheets. Wind howled like the voice of every root and river, every creature and stone.

Mother Earth had answered.

The sword gleamed with both Solara's fire and Lena's calm.

And the reckoning had begun.

* * *

Chapter 3 - The Heart of the Storm

Malrik's scream echoed through the storm, rattling branches and curling smoke through the spring air. The trees moaned as if responding, their leaves shivering with an instinct older than memory.

From the convoy, his goons poured out—hulking men in black, eyes hard, jaws clenched. They stormed toward the meadow with force and certainty, unaffected by rain, seemingly fueled by rage. Solara stood before them, Starcleave lit like a sunburst in her hand, but she did not strike.

The sword did something else.

As the first of the men neared the outer rim of the meadow, the light met them—not as fire, but as truth. One stopped mid-step. He blinked. His weapon drooped to his side. Another fell to his knees, staring at his own hands, unsure why they shook.

Hatred drained from their faces. Confusion replaced it. Tears, in some. Silence, in others.

The sword was changing them. Not attacking. Replacing.

Malrik had underestimated the sword.

He'd expected brute force. Fire and metal. But what met his men on the edge of the meadow was not destruction—it was revelation. The sword, pulsing with ancient energy, stripped away malice like mist in the sun. The closer his goons came, the more uncertain they became. One stopped mid-step, another lowered his weapon, blinking as if waking from a dream. Hatred turned to confusion, for some, remorse.

Malrik watched, fury boiling from beneath his cloak. He hissed through clenched teeth and stormed forward, shoving past his own dazed enforcers. Solara turned to meet him, Starcleave humming louder now, light spilling across the grass.

He slowed when he neared it. The glow cast shadows across his face, revealing the deep scars of his past—his wickedness etched not just in skin, but soul.

Still, he moved toward Lena.

Solara stepped in front of him.

"This ends here," she said, holding the sword with both hands.

Malrik hesitated. The blade trembled as if sensing the depth of his darkness. It flared, trying to purge, to reveal—but Malrik's evil was old. Woven into him.

He recoiled at the heat but did not fall.

With a roar, he lunged—not at Solara—but at Lena.

He grabbed her, wrapping a clawed hand around her arm.

"No!" Solara shouted, lunging forward, the sword slicing air—but not fast enough.

From the hillside above, Erik saw it all through his drone camera. His voice cracked over the headset. "There's something coming!"

He had seen the pressure shift on his screens, the funnel form above the tree line. It wasn't a storm—it was a force. A twisting column of wind and light, thick with leaves and whispers.

A tornado, but not. Not wrath. Will.

It struck the meadow like god's breath.

Malrik and Lena were swallowed in a blink. The funnel rose, lifted, spun—and then, silence.

Malrik was gone.

Lena lay in the grass, wrapped in roots, her chest barely moving.

Erik ran. He tore through the trees, leapt into the clearing, and dropped beside her.

"Hang on," he whispered, his voice breaking.

The roots loosened. The earth let her go. He lifted her gently, holding her like something too precious to lose.

Solara fell to her knees beside him. Lucy pressed in, nose to Lena's cheek. Uno stood behind them, calm but ready, his presence a wall of strength.

They gathered in a circle—Solara, Erik, Lucy, Uno—around the girl who had called Mother Earth to war.

The sky cleared. The sword dimmed.

The world, for a moment, exhaled.

* * *

Chapter 4 – The Eye of Reckoning

Inside the vortex, there was no time. No sound. Only pressure, and light, and an unraveling.

Malrik thrashed against the winds, his robes torn away, the layers of illusion and armor peeling from him like old skin. He screamed—not in rage, but in terror. The storm wasn't destroying him.

It was seeing him.

The magic he had hoarded for centuries, the darkness he had fed on, began to slip from his fingers like water. He tried to summon it back, to call on the shadows that had always obeyed. But the light in the storm—ancient, knowing—found every hidden corner of his soul and laid it bare.

He fell inward.

Visions overtook him. Faces of those he had crushed. Children whose names he'd never known. The weight of every soul he had twisted, every whisper he had poisoned.

And then—emptiness.

His power cracked like ice underfoot.

The storm lifted him higher and higher, until even the Earth could no longer hear him scream. And then, with gentle finality, it dropped him.

Not onto a battlefield. Not into the sea.

Into isolation.

* * *

A place between places. A desert, barren and quiet, with no life but stone and sky. He lay there, gasping, barely more than a man.

His magic gone. His voice silenced. His body broken. But alive.

And across the world, something shifted.

In cities and strongholds, in quiet rooms and corporate towers, the tendrils of Malrik's influence began to wane. His agents—men and women once steeped in his will—paused mid-sentence, mid-lie, mid-act.

They blinked.

They remembered.

A journalist in New York put down her pen, tears falling for a truth she'd long forgotten. A general in a bunker stood up and walked away from a war table. A scientist at a government lab erased a file filled with secrets no one should ever use.

All across the world, the light that had been stolen returned.

Not in blinding flashes, but in moments of clarity.

Malrik had not died.

But his reach had.

And the world, for the first time in a long time, remembered how to breathe.

* * *

PART 6: THE LIGHT REMAINS

Chapter 1 – Return to the Hive

Erik's fingers trembled on the wheel as the road unwound before them, gravel crunching beneath the tires. The storm had passed, but its memory lingered like static in the air. In the back seat, Lena lay nestled beneath a wool blanket, her skin pale but peaceful. Lucy lay atop her chest, head tucked beneath her chin, watching everything through narrowed, protective eyes.

Solara followed on Uno, her pace slow but unwavering. She kept to the tree line, letting Erik lead the way. The sword, now sheathed but glowing softly, remained at her side.

They reached the farm by dusk.

Erik's wife, Marian, stood in the doorway. The moment she saw Lena, her hand flew to her heart. "Bring her here," she said. No hesitation. No questions.

The house smelled of beeswax and bread, of lavender and oak. Marian took Lena into her arms like she had always belonged. Lucy followed, tail flicking like a guardian spirit.

Erik's friends—the Outliers—were collected around their own screens, replaying the storm, the light, the transformation. No one spoke for a long time. They didn't need to.

Solara stepped forward, her gaze steady. "I must return. My home... needs me, but Lena must be whole again".

Erik nodded slowly. "The sword?"

"It stays," Solara replied. "Its power remains on Earth. But it can only be activated when Lena and I are together. And Lena must stay here. She belongs to this world."

Together, they devised a plan. Erik's lab would become its sanctuary. They built a chamber beneath the greenhouse, wrapped in organic shielding and cloaked by layers of Erik's satellite tech. The sword's pulse would be masked, its energy signature scrambled to appear as soil data.

And so it was done.

* * *

One month passed.

The bees buzzed. The tomatoes climbed their cages. Marian

taught Lena to make soap and braid sweetgrass. Lena sang again—quietly at first, then freely, her voice rising with the wind. Her room faced east, where the sun warmed the orchard first. She had found a home. A family. A place to grow.

* * *

Solara watched from the ridge.

She waited until the stars were bright and the wind still.

She mounted Uno, her armor traded for travel cloth, the sword left in its cradle of roots and code beneath the Earth.

She took one last look at the house, the fields, the girl who had changed everything.

Then she whispered, "Home."

Uno galloped.

Faster.

The wind caught them. The stars bent.

And as they reached the speed of starlight, they disappeared—

—into dust and fire, returning to the sky that had once sent her forth.

* * *

Solara of Sardon

* * *

Epilogue– The Light Remains

Seasons turned gently.

The meadow where Solara and Lena met bloomed even brighter that year. Birds nested in the branches above the pond, and the moss beneath the roots pulsed with a quiet hum. No monument marked the place—only wildflowers and a stillness that welcomed those who listened.

On Erik's farm, honey flowed richly from the hives, and the fields sang with life. Lena, now a little stronger and a little taller, ran barefoot through the rows, Lucy always near, never straying far. She had found more than safety. She had found belonging.

Erik's wife often paused in her work to watch Lena sing to the trees or laugh in the sunlight. The girl's voice carried more than melody—it carried memory, and hope, and the pulse of a planet beginning to heal.

The sword, Starcleave, rested deep beneath the farm, wrapped in layers of living earth and clever shielding. Its energy quiet now, but not dormant. It waited not for battle, but for balance. For unity.

Somewhere far away—where storms no longer roared and machines no longer worked—Malrik stirred in silence. Weakened. Disconnected. And though the darkness still clung to him, the light he once feared now lived in every corner of the world. In kindness rekindled. In hearts reopened.

The Outliers—Erik's quiet circle of minds and magic—monitored what they could. The world was not saved in a single storm, but it had remembered itself. That was enough.

And sometimes, just before dawn, a few would look to the sky and swear they saw a streak of starlight—two forms, one of strength and one of loyalty, racing between dimensions.

Solara and Uno.

Not gone.

Just watching.

Just ready.

For the light, once awakened, never truly leaves.

Character Guide and Map of Sardon

Solara of Sardon

The last warrior of a dying world, Solara was born beneath a purple eclipse during the Crimson War. Fierce, compassionate, and guided by ancestral magic, she is bound to protect Earth and the children who call out in need. She wields the ancient sword Starcleave, seeded with the power of Sardon and awakened by Earth's rhythm.

Lena

A wild-hearted eight-year-old girl with round green eyes and the blood of the Veil in her veins. Born of Earth, but deeply connected to ancient magic, Lena is the missing balance that completes Starcleave. She sees the truth in things and carries the wisdom of the forest within her.

Uno

A mystical white stallion found frozen in time during Sardon's darkest hour. Bonded to Solara through spirit and silence, Uno carries her across worlds and battles, embodying freedom, loyalty, and quiet strength.

Lucy

A small but fierce Jack Russell Terrier with wiry fur and boundless courage. Lucy is Lena's protector and guide, leading her through the forest and back into the arms of destiny. Unshakably loyal and brave beyond measure.

Erik Halden

A scientist and reluctant mystic, Erik leads the Outliers—a secretive network tracking cosmic disturbances and magical anomalies. Grounded and analytical, he becomes an unlikely ally in Solara's quest to shield Earth's magic from darkness.

Bran

An ancient guide in the Grove of Breath and Bone. Part sage, part spirit, Bran tends to the sacred ley lines and carries the last memories of the ancestors. He prepares Solara to receive Earth's half of Starcleave's awakening.

Malrik

Once a brilliant seer, now a corrupted sorcerer twisted by centuries of shadow magic. He commands the Huskborn and seeks dominion over life and death. Though his body was unmade in the Eye of Reckoning, a remnant of him may still linger in the folds of time.

The Huskborn

Elite warriors forged from broken men—mercenaries, soldiers, exiles—stripped of mercy and memory. Enhanced by Malrik's dark alchemy, they serve without question, weapons of wrath and silence.

The Outliers

A clandestine group monitoring magical disruptions and protecting Earth's unseen thresholds. Led by Erik Halden, they work behind the veil to guard Starcleave and Lena, balancing science and myth.

* * *

www.ingramcontent.com/pod-product-compliance
Lightning Source LLC
Chambersburg PA
CBHW070752180626
46818CB00007B/3085